The C.R. Gibson Company,
Norwalk, Connecticut 06856

What on Earth are You Doing, for Heaven's Sake?

Illustrated by Bron Smith

Christians are the light of the world, but the switch has to be turned on.

Jesus still makes house calls.

Trying times are the times
to try more faith.

If your trouble is long-standing
try kneeling.

Sorrow looks back.
Worry looks around.
Faith looks up.

Patience is a virtue that carries a lot of wait.

Triumph is "umph" added to try.

Interested in going to Heaven?
Get your flight training here.

Redemption Center.
No stamps needed.

Come as you are.
God will have you
no other way.

Let the Son shine in!

Let gratitude be
your attitude.

Prayer is the next best
thing to being there.

The Christian is tallest
when on his knees.

A lot of kneeling will keep
you in good standing with God.

Temptation is sure to ring your doorbell, but it's your fault if you ask it to stay for dinner.

Seven days without prayer makes one weak.

You alone can do it, but you can't do it alone.

DING!
DONG!

Read the Bible...
Prevent Truth decay.

Get the "New Look"
from the "Old Book".

you can't break God's promises
by leaning on them.

Faith is to the soul what
a main spring is to a watch.

No God,
No peace.
Know God,
Know peace.

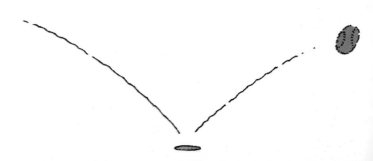

Have fun
in the Son...
you won't burn.

No light shines brighter
than the Son.

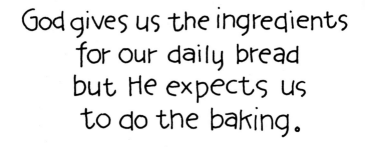

Wearing your halo too tight also gives others a headache.

Blowing out the other person's candle won't make yours any brighter.

When a person has a pet peeve, it's amazing how often he pets it.

A man wrapped up in himself
makes a very small parcel.

God is not permissive. If he were, we would have the Ten Suggestions!

The Ten Commandments are not multiple choice.

Form good habits... They are just as hard to break as bad ones.

Christians aren't perfect... just forgiven!

A man can't stumble
when he's on his knees.

A closed heart can only be
opened from the inside.